Something Goes Wrong in the Waldorff Kitchen

LORETTA A. JOHNSON

Illustrations by KRISTEN M. JURGENS

Copyright © 2015 Loretta A. Johnson.

All rights reserved. No part of this book may be used or reproduced by any means, graphic, electronic, or mechanical, including photocopying, recording, taping or by any information storage retrieval system without the written permission of the author except in the case of brief quotations embodied in critical articles and reviews.

This is a work of fiction. All of the characters, names, incidents, places, organizations, and dialogue in this novel are either the products of the author's imagination or are used fictitiously.

Archway Publishing books may be ordered through booksellers or by contacting:

Archway Publishing
1663 Liberty Drive
Bloomington, IN 47403
www.archwaypublishing.com
1 (888) 242-5904

Because of the dynamic nature of the Internet, any web addresses or links contained in this book may have changed since publication and may no longer be valid. The views expressed in this work are solely those of the author and do not necessarily reflect the views of the publisher, and the publisher hereby disclaims any responsibility for them.

Any people depicted in stock imagery provided by Thinkstock are models, and such images are being used for illustrative purposes only.
Certain stock imagery © Thinkstock.

ISBN: 978-1-4808-2420-1 (sc)
ISBN: 978-1-4808-2419-5 (e)

Print information available on the last page.

Archway Publishing rev. date: 11/3/2015

Dedications:

Let me start by giving God the Glory, Honor and Praise for inspiring me to write this story and waking me up in the wee hours of the morning to get it completed.

To my loving Mother Mrs. Dollie Thomas who gave me the right tools of life to fulfill my destiny.

My 3 Son's...Isaiah, Samuel and Silas, II whom I love dearly.

Mrs. Emma Taylor, friend and prayer partner from start until...

preface:

I began writing Something Goes Wrong In The Waldorff Kitchen on December 4, 2014. It all started with a vision, a prayer, an imagination, a piece of paper and the stroke of a pen. It was not written in a day. However, over a period of time and many times writing on whatever was available whether it was a napkin, paper sack, piece of fabric, scrapes, Sunday's Church Programs, a menu, etc...it started to come together in my mind the characters, the time, the place, the setting and all those loose pieces of papers and what have you. "The book was finally written!"

Loretta shouts out a Big "Thank You," and hope that her readers enjoy reading the book as well as she enjoyed writing it. There were times I giggled myself she says. "Chow!" Means good-bye.

The Author will make a charitable donation to the following organizations for each book sold:

Springfield Boys & Girls Club

Sojourn Women and Children's Shelter

Operation Homefront
(Supporting our troops and helping the families they leave behind)

Acknowledgements:

Hats off to my Illustrator Ms. Kristen M. Jurgens, Art Teacher of Lanphier High School in Springfield, Illinois. Thank you from the bottom of my heart for your commitment in bringing the book to life. Your skills were a necessary piece and I appreciate your dedication and services. When it's game time I will sit with the Southeast Spartans, the High School I graduated from. LOL!!! Kristen also is the owner of Art & Soul paint parties and more...Check out her website at: www.artandsoulspirit.com

To my Editors Ms. Leslie Thomas, Communications and Mrs. Martha Jordan, Teacher. Thank you ladies for making sure I dotted all my i's – crossed all my t's and checked my spelling. "Great Job!"

Thank you to Mr. Chris Wills, Public Information Officer for permission to use the Abraham Lincoln Presidential Library and Museum featured inside the book.

Thank you to Archway Publishing FROM SIMON & SCHUSTER for being there from start to finish. Your support team was awesome! You've allowed me to fulfil my dream and reach for the star with my name on it that the light that shines within me will inspire and enlighten the lives of children and the young in heart everywhere. More books to come...

Introduction:

"The Famous Waldorff Le' Grand"
Restaurant

Chefs Louie & Pierre

Ages 4-8

The King and Queen of the Emerald Crystal Palace plan to dine at The Famous Waldorff Le' Grand during their visit to Springfield, Illinois. Chefs Louie and Pierre are excited and try to prepare for the night in order to make it perfect. The staff of the Waldorff must work together to avoid serving a disastrous dinner. Hey, kids! Ask a grown-up to help you make the delicious snacks located toward the end of the book. "Have fun reading and enjoy!"

Chefs Louie and Pierre Waldorff, two brothers born in France and later USA citizens in the city of Springfield, Illinois. One day the brothers decided to open up a Restaurant named the Famous Waldorff Le' Grand.

Everyday Chef Louie would receive and open the mail! One very normal day, a very sleek, and gold embellished envelope arrived. As Chef Louie carefully read the important looking mail he began to scream... "Pierre! Pierre! We've just received a formal announcement from the Emerald Crystal Palace of the City of Alabaster! You'll never guess who it's from?" Chef Louie eager with excitement presents the announcement to his brother Pierre.

King George & Queen Anna
of
Crystal Palace of Alabaster
will be arriving in Springfield, Illinois
for a short visit to tour the
Abraham Lincoln Presidential Library & Museum
They have requested to dine at the
Famous Waldorff Le' Grand
on June 11th

The announcement read; King George and Queen Anna of the Emerald Crystal Palace of Alabaster will be arriving in Springfield, Illinois for a short visit to tour the Abraham Lincoln Presidential Library and Museum. They have requested to dine at the "Famous Waldorff Le' Grand," on June 11th.

"Oh my, Louie, we must make haste to prepare for the King and Queen's royal arrival; said Pierre! "This calls for our finest choice selections from top to bottom for this special occasion! "I will meet with the kitchen staff," said Louie. "And I will get started on a signature menu masterpiece fit for royalty," said Pierre as they hurried off.

-Le' Menu Royale-

Crowned Lamb
Chicken with Waldorff Specialty Sauce
Salmon in a Garden

Diamond Glazed Carrots
Dancing Peas with Pimentos
Ratatouille
Potatoes Divine
Waldorff Signature Salad
Croissants/French Bread/Crackers
Brie Cheese

-Desserts-

Sparkling Crème Brulee with Walnuts
Raspberry/Blackberry Crepes
Waldorff Signature Cake
Mixed Jeweled Fruit

-Specialty Teas-

Within minutes, Pierre completes a scrumptious and superb menu...

...while Louie finishes giving final instructions on the décor in the dining area.

The next morning Pierre places an order with the towns local Meat, Poultry and Seafood Company-owned by three generations.

The local Meat, Poultry and Seafood Company made their early morning deliveries as usual. First stop was to Casey's Dine In – Carry Out Restaurant. Mr. Casey signs off on his order and bids the driver good-bye. The next route was to the Famous Waldorff Le' Grand Restaurant. Pierre signs off on his order and bids the driver farewell.

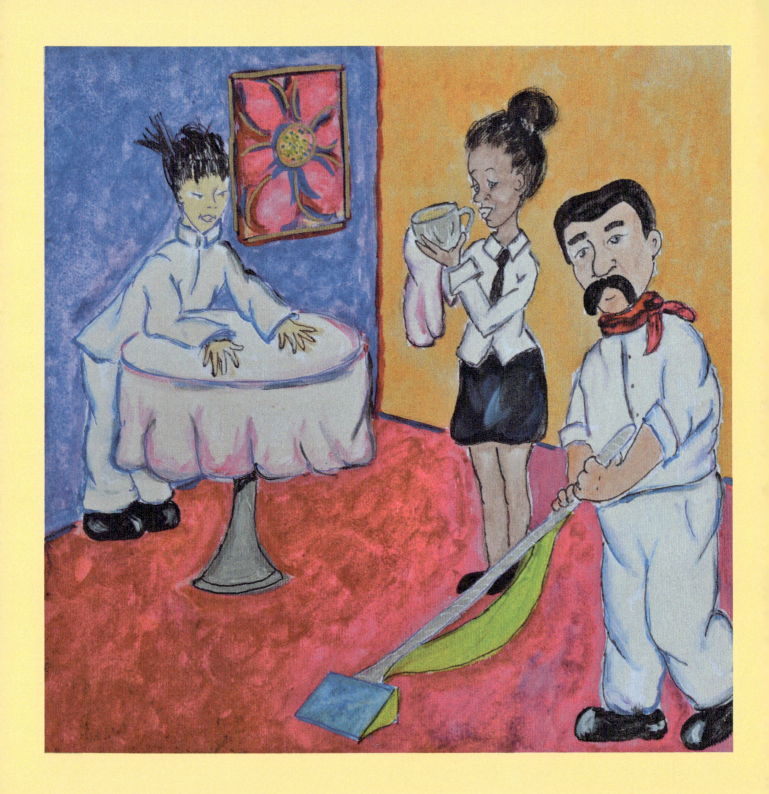

The Waldorff staff lines up to receive final instructions. Pierre *shouts*, "FIRE UP THE OVENS!" Louie *orders* everyone to polish all the silver, pull out the fine china, and set the tables. "*Make haste!*" Pierre commands.

Meanwhile... Bernard, the Waldorff's assistant chef, looks over the menu with confusion and tells the head cooks; Kim, Charmaine, Ron and Alberto that there has been a change in the menu. Pierre ordered chitterlings instead of lamb. "Does anybody know how to prepare them?" asked Bernard. They all answered, *"No!"* Chef Bernard said," This is a new specialty meat and must be prepared to *perfection.*" He ordered that they pull out the Waldorff cookbooks and find out how to prepare the chitterlings.

They retrieved all their secret recipes, but could not find one for the chitterlings. Then they went through all the cook books. Confused, puzzled and exhausted, they almost gave up, when Charmaine said, "I know what we need to do! Let me call my Grandmother," There's nothing she can't cook." And Charmaine did just that.

As the other cooks looked on in amazement Charmaine's Grandmother came to the rescue and instructed her on how to prepare the chitterlings. Charmaine forwarded the information to all the head cooks and to Chef Bernard. They all jumped up and shouted, "HOORAY!"

The King and Queen's Limo arrived as scheduled. "Welcome to our fine city of Springfield, Illinois King George and Queen Anna," said Pierre. "We do hope your travel was a pleasant one," said Louie, as they both bowed in respect. "Indeed it was my good fellow," the King responded and the Queen smiled as they were escorted into the Famous Waldorff Le' Grand.

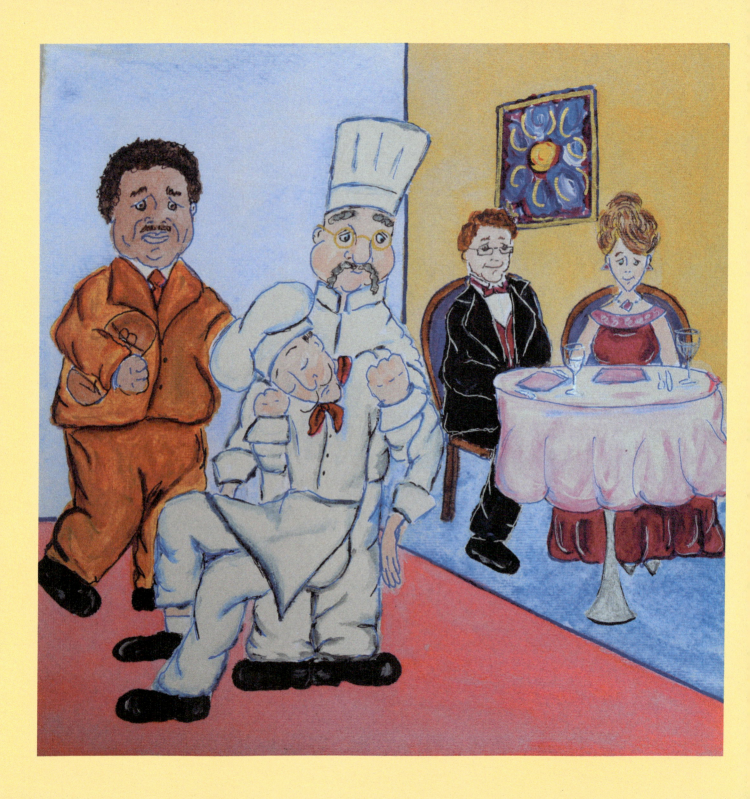

The waiters and waitresses began serving the King and Queen in unison as the violin trio began playing soft dinner music. Mr. Casey, clutching a package under his arm, enters the restaurant in a hurry and walks over to Pierre and Louie. While he explains the mix-up, Pierre was shocked and fainted into Louie's arms. Meanwhile, Mr. Casey and Louie, astonished, look on as the King and Queen are served *chitterlings*.

King George takes a bite and begins to chew. He chewed and he chewed. Pierre awakens to hear King George express his delight in this particular dish. "Why I have never enjoyed something so comforting and satisfying to my soul," the King said softly. He looks at Queen Anna and says, "How about you my lady?" She replied that the entire meal was indeed delightful and scrumptious!

Chefs Pierre and Louie were pleased and overcome with joy that the dinner was not a disaster, as they all escorted the Royal Guest toward their waiting Limousine. King George said "when we visit your good city of Springfield, Illinois again do have the *chitterlings* waiting for me." Queen Anna agreed and smiled graciously. Mr. Casey suggested that they try hot sauce on them with coleslaw on the side next time. The King happily replied, "I will my good fellow, I will." King George and Queen Anna waived good-bye as their limousine headed toward the Abraham Lincoln Presidential Library and Museum.

Pierre and Louie thanked Mr. Casey and asked him to join them for a cup of coffee back inside the Famous Waldorff Le' Grand and he did.

The End

Waldorff's Gooey Sandwich Cookies

(Lil' Chefs ask an adult to help you with this recipe)

1 – Ready to bake Chocolate Chip Cookie Dough **(in the refrigerator section)**

1 - Jar Marshmallow Crème

Prepare *refrigerated cookie dough according to directions on the package. After cookies have cooled –* **Spread** *marshmallow crème on the bottom side of one cookie, then put a lid on it with another cookie. You now have completed one sandwich cookie. Repeat with the remaining batch.* **"Delicious!"**

Waldorff's Healthy Carrot Crunch Snack

(Lil' Chefs ask an adult to help you with this recipe)

1 or 2 – Slices of Bread

1 – Pkg. of Cream Cheese **(softened)**

1 – Bag of Shredded Carrots

Toast your bread, then **spread** cream cheese on top and **cover** with the shredded carrots. Cut in triangle half's. **Yum! Yum!**

Note: The Nutrition label will appear on the back of all your ingredients.

CPSIA information can be obtained at www.ICGtesting.com
Printed in the USA
BVOW07s1912201115

427806BV00026B/174/P

9 781480 824201